DATE DUE		

tle.

sed

Sis-

ith

're

d.

ou

is

n

BIG CHAPTER BOOKS

The Berenstain Bears

AND THE G-REX BONES

by the Berenstains

A BIG CHAPTER BOOK™

Random House 🏠 New York

www.randomhouse.com/kids
www.berenstainbears.com

Library of Congress Cataloging-in-Publication Data
Berenstain, Stan, 1923-
The Berenstain Bears and the G-Rex bones / by the Berenstains.
p. cm. — (A big chapter book)
Summary: Doctor Zoltan Bearish and his gang of swindlers try to pass off fake dinosaur bones in order to embarrass Professor Actual Factual and the Bearsonian Institution.
ISBN 0-679-88945-0 (trade). — ISBN 0-679-98945-5 (lib. bdg.)
[1. Bears—Fiction. 2. Dinosaurs—Fiction. 3. Fossils—Fiction. 4. Swindlers and swindling—Fiction.] I. Berenstain, Jan, 1923-   . II. Title. III. Series: Berenstain, Stan, 1923- . Big chapter book.
PZ7.B4483Befc   1999 [Fic]—dc21 98-29559

Printed in the United States of America   10 9 8 7 6 5 4 3 2 1

BIG CHAPTER BOOKS is a trademark of Berenstain Enterprises, Inc.

Contents

Chapter 1
An Unexpected Visitor

Ralph Ripoff, Beartown's small-time crook and swindler, had just settled down to an afternoon nap on his houseboat's living room sofa when there was a knock at the front door.

"Who could that be?" Ralph said to himself.

"Who could that be? Who could that be?" said his pet parrot, Squawk, ever alert on his perch by the window that looked out on the river.

Ralph ignored Squawk and padded to the door. He opened it. There stood a tall, thin bear who looked vaguely familiar.

"Zoltan Bearish," said the visitor in a deep voice. He had dark eyes and a piercing gaze. He wore a long black coat and a black wide-brimmed hat.

"No, sir," answered Ralph. "I'm Ralph Ripoff. I don't know any Zoltan Bearish."

"You do now," said the bear, with a little smile.

"I do?" said Ralph. "How's that?"

"Because *I* am Zoltan Bearish," said the bear. "*Doctor* Zoltan Bearish."

"Oh, I get it," said Ralph, chuckling at the misunderstanding. "But I didn't know doctors made house calls anymore. Especially when you don't even ask them to come."

"I am not a medical doctor, Mr. Ripoff," said Bearish patiently. "I am a doctor of chemistry."

"Oh, is that so?" said Ralph. "Well, what can I do for you, Doctor?"

"First, you can invite me in," said Bearish. His gaze became even more penetrating.

Ralph didn't usually invite callers in before they had stated their business. But Dr. Bearish's gaze had gained a strange hold on him. "Please come in," he heard himself say.

When they had seated themselves in the living room, Ralph said, "You look familiar, Doctor. Have you ever lived in Beartown?"

"Yes," said Bearish. He sat stiffly, his long, thin hands folded in his lap. "About five years ago I worked in the laboratory at the Bearsonian Institution. I was the head chemist. In fact, I was the *only* chemist."

"Sounds like a lonely job," said Ralph.

"Not at all," replied Bearish. "An assistant would only have gotten on my nerves. After all, I am the finest chemist in all Bear Country."

"If you don't say so yourself," chuckled Ralph. Boy, was this guy weird! "How come you left Beartown?"

Dr. Bearish's smile vanished. His gaze drifted to the window. "The Bearsonian director and I had a...a falling out, you might say." His use of the phrase "falling out" brought the smile back to his face for a moment, for it had caused him to imagine a certain bear falling out of an upper-story Bearsonian window.

"The director," said Ralph. "You mean Professor Actual Factual?"

Suddenly, Dr. Bearish sat bolt upright in his chair. "Don't *ever* say that name in my presence!" he snapped.

Ralph shrank back into the sofa. "Sorry, Doctor," he mumbled. This guy was an even bigger weirdo than he'd thought! "Guess that means he fired you?"

"That is correct," admitted Bearish. "It was over the most trivial of matters. I accidentally left the lid off a container of experimental fruit flies."

"It must have been a pretty important experiment for the professor to fire you for that," said Ralph.

"Hardly!" snapped Bearish again, making Ralph jump. "He was only angry because the flies ate the apple he'd brought for his lunch."

Ralph nodded. But if he hadn't been trying to be polite, he would have shaken his head instead. He knew Professor Actual Factual pretty well. And he knew that the professor was not only the greatest scientist in the history of Bear Country, but also one of its kindest, most generous citizens. Firing someone over a lost lunch just wasn't his style.

"In any event," continued Dr. Bearish, "I've come to you for assistance in seeking justice. I have devised a swindle to get back at the professor-who-shall-remain-nameless. Unfortunately, I have no practical experience in the swindling department."

"Well, you've come to the right place," said Ralph, holding his arms out wide. "The Department of Swindles—Ralph Ripoff, director, at your service. Let's hear your plan."

Dr. Bearish relaxed his gaze and leaned back in his chair. "You may know," he began, "that the professor-who-shall-remain-nameless has long sought a particular fossil skeleton to complete his collection in the Bearsonian Hall of Dinosaurs."

"You mean a *T-rex* skeleton?" said Ralph. "Sure, everyone in Beartown knows that. He even built that special room to put it in when he finds one."

"The rotunda," said Bearish.

Ralph had never heard the word before

but thought it was a perfect one for the big circular room with the high domed ceiling that Actual Factual had built.

"After five long years of experiments in my private laboratory in Big Bear City," continued Bearish, "I have at last produced a substance that can be shaped into perfect fake fossils. It can be made cheaply and in large amounts. And chemical analysis will reveal no difference between it and real fossil material, which I had a chance to study in detail in the Bearsonian lab."

"Don't tell me," said Ralph. "You want to

make a fake *T-rex* skeleton and sell it to the Bearsonian for a million dollars. See, I'm one step ahead of you, Doctor."

"More like half a step," said Bearish. "Because I've already had the fossil bones made—by a sculptor who is tired of being poor. And they aren't *T-rex* bones. They are the bones of a similar but as yet undiscovered species twice the size of *T-rex*. Imagine: *twice* the size! It will barely fit into the rotunda of the Hall of Dinosaurs. I figure this skeleton will bring at least five times as much money as a *T-rex* skeleton."

"What do you call this new dinosaur species?" asked Ralph.

"I don't," said Bearish. "We'll sweeten the deal by allowing the professor to name it himself."

"He oughta love that," said Ralph. "Get his name into the *National Bearographic* again. But there's one thing I don't understand, Doctor. How exactly would you get back at the professor with this swindle? You'll make a lot of money, of course, but the professor will make an even bigger name for himself in the science world than he has already."

Dr. Bearish smiled an evil little smile. "Very simple," he said. "Exactly one year after the sale of the fossil skeleton to the Bearsonian, I shall go to the media and reveal the hoax. The professor will be completely humiliated over having been tricked

in a matter of science. His reputation will be stained forever."

Now, most bears wouldn't have understood why Dr. Bearish could reveal the hoax after a year without fear of being arrested and thrown in jail. But no one was better versed in the ins and outs of hoaxes, swindles, and other kinds of fraud than Ralph Ripoff. He knew that a victim of fraud had to report the crime to the police within one year of the commission of the crime. If the victim failed to do so, the swindler could not be arrested and tried in a court of law for the crime—ever. It was called a "statute of limitations"—a law limiting the amount of time for reporting a crime. And to Ralph Ripoff, statutes of limitations were the most beautiful laws in all the land.

"As far as it goes," said Ralph, "it's ingenious. But if your fake fossils are as good as you say they are, why would anyone believe you about the hoax?"

"Ah," said Bearish. "I have marked one of the fossil leg bones with a chemical symbol known only to me. A kind of chemical signature. I will direct the media to examine and identify it with the help of chemists."

Dr. Bearish's penetrating gaze bore into Ralph's eyes. *He's trying to hypnotize me,* thought Ralph. *This mad scientist is trying to trick me into helping him with his evil plan!*

And evil it was. Cheating the Bearsonian out of millions of dollars wasn't what was bothering Ralph, of course. After all, taking other bears' hard-earned money was the lifeblood of swindlers. But usually there was nothing *personal* about it. Destroying the hard-earned reputation of a good and kind bear was different. A bear's reputation was

worth more than any amount of money.

Ralph knew from his days as a carnival hypnotist that a bear couldn't be hypnotized if he didn't want to be. *I won't let him do this to me,* he thought as he fought Dr. Bearish's gaze for control over his own mind. *Ralph Ripoff swindles only those bears he wants to swindle!*

That's when Zoltan Bearish lost the battle for Ralph's mind. But, oddly enough, that didn't make Ralph refuse to take part in the doctor's evil scheme. You see, most bears, like most humans, have a strong urge to do the selfish thing. And, as you can probably tell from his whole career, Ralph had never had much success resisting that urge. What's more, as you will see from his thoughts below, Ralph had a knack for turning what was good for Ralph into what was good for everyone.

Now wait a minute, thought Ralph. *There's a downside to Bearish's scheme, but it also has an upside.* He, Ralph, would be famous! In his mind's eye, he pictured his own smiling face on the cover of *Swindler's Digest.* Across it were the words: The Greatest. Why, Ralph's Place would become a swindlers' shrine! Crooks and conbears from all over Bear Country would flock to it to pay their respects. And he could receive them at his leisure, for the million dollars or so he would get from the swindle would mean he'd never have to swindle anyone again for the rest of his life. Indeed, Actual Factual's loss would be everyone else's gain. By helping Zoltan Bearish, he would be doing good for all bearkind!

Besides, thought Ralph, *Actual Factual is supposed to be the greatest scientist in Bear Country history. If he hurts his reputation by allowing himself to be the victim of a scientific hoax, he'll have only himself to blame, won't he?*

Blaming the victim: that was another thing Ralph did even more often than most bears. It was natural in his line of work.

"Dr. Bearish," said Ralph, "I have considered your plan and found it good. For twenty percent of the take, I'll help you get your revenge."

"Agreed," said Bearish. "But I prefer to call it justice."

"Sounds more like revenge to me," muttered Ralph.

"Revenge, justice," said Bearish with a shrug. "Is there a difference?"

Chapter 2
Swindle Within a Swindle

Even a crook like Ralph Ripoff thought that Zoltan Bearish's idea of justice was a little spooky. But not spooky enough to make him change his mind about collecting a million dollars.

What Bearish needed was someone to organize the whole plan. And Ralph certainly filled the bill. Even before they shook hands on the deal, Ralph's mind was hard at work. First he had to hire someone to "discover" the phony fossils in a likely place.

And Ralph knew just the bear for the job. His name was Sandcrab Jones, and he lived all alone in a little shack out in Great Grizzly Desert, a good fifty miles west of Beartown. Sandcrab would strike fossil gold while pretending to dig a deep well in the dry streambed near his shack. Then Ralph would contact the media, who would broadcast live the rest of the skeleton being dug up. With good planning and execution, no one would suspect a hoax.

Now, Sandcrab Jones was an old hermit who had probably never had more than a few dollars in his pocket at any one time. Ralph knew that he could get him to do the job for as little as twenty or thirty dollars. Of course, he wouldn't tell Dr. Bearish that. He'd say that Sandcrab had demanded two hundred dollars, and when Bearish gave him the money to pay Sandcrab, he'd give Sandcrab the twenty or thirty they'd agreed on and keep the rest for himself. He'd do the same thing—pull the same swindle within a swindle—with the Bogg Brothers, whose labor and pickup truck he'd hire to transport the fake fossils to the desert. These career crooks lived in an old run-down house in Forbidden Bog. They were a lot smarter than Sandcrab Jones, but Ralph suspected they didn't know the true value of dinosaur fossils. Ralph figured he could get

their truck and labor for about two hundred dollars. But he'd tell Dr. Bearish that they had demanded *five* hundred, and he'd pocket the difference, just as he'd do with Sandcrab Jones.

Yes, the scheme was not only foolproof but highly profitable. In a year's time Ralph would be a millionaire, and in the meantime his little swindles on the side would buy him all the food, spats, straw hats, and canes he'd need until the big swindle finally paid off.

Chapter 3
Watched?

Ralph wasted no time putting his plan into action. And it worked like a charm—at least, up to the point of burying the dinosaur bones. There were so many of them and they were so big that the Bogg Brothers had to make three separate round trips to the desert in their pickup truck.

Finally, the third and final trip was almost done. The last shovels full of sandy streambed dirt had been tamped down over the buried dinosaur bones with the backs of

five shovels. The five bears holding the
shovels wiped their sweaty brows and
looked at one another with satisfaction.

"That crazy doctor will be pleased as heck

when I tell him these phony bones are safely in the ground," said Ralph Ripoff.

"Not half as pleased as I am," wheezed Sandcrab Jones, rubbing his aching old back.

The three Bogg Brothers, who were rubbing their backs too, nodded.

"You three have no right to complain," groused Ralph, "riding in that comfy cab while I bounced around with the bones in the back of the truck! Well, let's hit the road. See you tomorrow, Sandcrab, with an entire media crew."

Ralph handed the hermit thirty dollars.

"Thanks, sonny," said Sandcrab. "What did you say your name was again?"

"Ralph. Ralph Ripoff. You remember me, don't you? I'm the guy you bought that termite insurance from. Well, happy fossil huntin', old-timer."

"No time like the present, I guess," said Sandcrab, plunging the blade of his shovel into the newly tamped-down earth. But then he stopped and looked up. And looked all around.

"What's wrong?" asked Ralph.

"Maybe nothin'," said the old hermit. "But I just got a funny feelin' we're bein' watched. Right at this very moment."

Ralph looked all around. Even though they were standing in a shallow gulch where the streambed was, he could see for miles in every direction. And all he saw was sand, rocks, cactuses, and, in the distance, a few of those flat-topped reddish hills called mesas. He looked back into Sandcrab's blurry eyes. "Your eyesight is as bad as your memory, old-timer," he said. "There's no one out there."

"I didn't say I *saw* anyone out there," protested Sandcrab. "I said I had a *feelin'*."

"Well," said Ralph, "if we can't see them, they can't see us. Okay, we're outta here."

Ralph looked back at Sandcrab Jones from the back of the pickup as it followed its own sandy tire tracks back to the highway. "Feeble old guy," he said to himself. "All these years alone out here in the desert sun must have made him crazier than a bedbug."

Chapter 4
Seen

But Ralph was wrong about Sandcrab Jones. Dead wrong. Sandcrab was no crazier than you or I. And though his memory and eyesight *had* grown a bit feeble with age, he was the exact opposite of feeble in some other important ways. He had a kind of sixth sense about certain things. For instance, he could predict right to the minute when the rare, sudden desert rains would come. And he could always tell you, right to the day, when the big cactus outside his shack would push out its tiny pink flowers. And, like most bears who spend almost all their time alone, he always knew when he was being watched.

Just minutes before Sandcrab made his surprising statement, a small group of cubs was scanning the horizon with binoculars from the top of a mesa about a mile away. They were from Teacher Bob's and Teacher Jane's classes at Bear Country School in Beartown, and they were out in the desert on a nature hike. Twenty minutes earlier they had chased a roadrunner down into a gorge while the rest of the group drifted off. And now they were lost.

"I say we go east," said Brother Bear, lowering his binoculars.

"Why east?" asked Sister.

"I just remembered," said Brother. "When we started out, Teacher Bob said we

were headed west from the highway. Who's got a compass? I forgot mine."

"I forgot mine, too," said Sister.

"I left mine on the bus," said Lizzy Bruin. "It felt all lumpy in my pocket."

Brother looked hopefully at Cousin Fred. Surely a semi-nerd like Fred would bring a compass on a nature hike. But Fred felt in his pocket, only to pull it inside out with a sigh. There was a big hole in it.

"I've got mine!" said Barry Bruin.

Proudly he held it up for all to see. It was tiny. Sort of a baby compass. Barry looked at it and frowned. He shook it and looked again. "Darn!" he said. "It's busted!"

"Where did you get that crummy little thing, anyway?" said Sister.

"From a box of Grizzly Jack," said Barry. "It was the prize. It must have broken when I bit it by accident."

"Great!" said Sister. "*You're* a prize, too, Barry."

"So how do we figure out which way east is?" asked Lizzy.

"I know!" said Fred. "The sun! It rises in the east and sets in the west!"

Shading their eyes, they all looked up. And groaned in unison. The sun was directly overhead.

"That means it's noon!" cried Barry.

"So what?" said Sister.

Barry shrugged. "So, at least we know what time it is."

More groans.

"We're saved!" cried Fred all of a sudden. He pointed at the spot his binoculars were aimed at. "I see the bus! We're only about a mile from the highway. Let's get going."

The cubs headed for the highway side of the mesa. But then they held back. "Come on, Liz!" called Barry.

Lizzy hadn't budged. She was training her binoculars on something far off in the opposite direction. The others hurried to

her side. "What is it, Liz?" asked Brother.

"I see some bears out there," she said. "In a shallow gulch. Look."

They scanned the area Lizzy was aiming at until they all found the bears.

"Five of 'em," said Fred. "And there's a pickup truck at the edge of the gulch."

"They're all holding something," said Sister. "Shovels, I think. Hey, one of them just looked up. Now he's looking all around. He's looking in this direction."

"Who are they?" Brother asked Lizzy, who had the sharpest eyesight of any of the cubs.

Lizzy peered extra hard through the rising heat waves that made everything wiggly and watery. "I can't make out any faces," she said. "But one of them is wearing a straw hat. Now he's looking around too. He's got a green suit on. And white things down around his ankles."

"Spats?" said Fred. "Green suit? Straw hat? You just described Ralph Ripoff."

"What the heck is Ralph doing way out here in the desert?" said Sister.

"Hmm," said Brother. "Something tells me that's for Ralph to know and us to find out."

"Does that mean you're gonna call a meeting of the Bear Detectives?" asked Fred eagerly.

"Not yet," said Brother. "We need more to go on. Maybe something will turn up in the next few days. Meanwhile, let's get back to the bus. Sooner or later Teacher Bob and Teacher Jane will look for us there."

Chapter 5
Fossil Furor

It turned out that Brother was right about both things. Teacher Bob and Teacher Jane did eventually check the bus for the lost cubs. And something did turn up about Ralph's desert trip in the next few days. The very *next* day, in fact.

The Bear family was gathered in front of the TV in the family room after dinner. Papa aimed the remote at the TV and pressed the on button. They were all very excited because they'd just gotten cable. Papa and Mama wanted to watch the Bear News Network (BNN), Brother wanted sports (BSPN), and Sister wanted Bear

Music Television (BMTV). But Papa was the supreme lord and master of the remote (at least, whenever Mama let him be). So on came BNN.

A *BNN-Live* telecast was in progress. On camera was some sandy ground, on which rested some very large bones. The camera shifted to a group of bears digging with shovels in the sandy earth.

"Hey, that's Dan Digger and his team of workbears," said Papa. "I wonder what they found."

Then came the voice of Christiane Aman-bear, the famous roving newscaster. "I'm out here in Great Grizzly Desert, where an old hermit named Sandcrab Jones has dis-covered fossils of a dinosaur near his shack."

The camera shifted to another very rec-ognizable bear, who was more infamous than famous. "Standing next to me," continued Amanbear, "is Ralph Ripoff, Beartown's well-known small-time crook and swindler. I understand, Mr. Ripoff, that Sandcrab Jones contacted you soon after he found the dinosaur bones. Is that correct?"

"That is correct, Christiane," said Ralph, grabbing the mike from her as he smiled broadly at the camera. "Sandcrab knew

there was going to be a lot of publicity from this, not to mention a little money, and he was worried about handling such complicated matters all by himself. So I agreed to be his agent. He and I go way back, you know."

"So I hear, Mr. Ripoff," said Amanbear, snatching back the mike. "Our research staff has found that some time ago you sold Sandcrab Jones a termite insurance policy for his shack. They also found that the

yearly price of the policy is more than it would cost Mr. Jones to rebuild his shack if it were completely destroyed by termites."

"Termites?" said Ralph nervously. "I thought we were gonna talk about dinosaurs, not termites."

"Maybe I should ask Mr. Jones himself about the termite insurance," said Amanbear. "Where is he?"

"He's holed up in his shack over yonder," said Ralph quickly. "Kinda camera-shy, you know..."

Papa hit the mute button and turned to Mama. "This is *really* big news," he said. "Did you see the size of those bones? Wait'll Professor Actual Factual hears about this!"

"I'm sure he already has, dear," said Mama. "But it bothers me that Ralph is involved..."

"Nonsense!" said Papa. "You heard Amanbear. Ralph sold Sandcrab some phony termite insurance. The old coot is probably feeble-minded. Natural for him to contact Ralph. Besides, there's no chance in the whole wide world that Ralph would try to swindle Actual Factual. The professor knows fossils through and through. And that includes knowing what they're worth."

"I guess you're right," said Mama. "Still..."

"What do you think, cubs?" said Papa. "Pretty exciting, eh?"

The cubs had been transfixed by the sight of Ralph Ripoff and bears with shovels in Great Grizzly Desert for the second day in a row. They were still staring at the TV screen.

"Who, me?" said Brother. "Sure, Dad, it's great. I think I'll go upstairs and do my homework now." He started up the stairs, then stopped and announced more loudly, "I said: I THINK I'LL GO UPSTAIRS AND DO MY HOMEWORK NOW..."

Sister jumped up. "Oh, yeah, me too," she said, and hurried after Brother to talk about what they had just seen on TV.

Chapter 6
Gigantosaurus rex!

By the time the Bear Detectives gathered in their usual booth at the Burger Bear the next evening, it was all over town that Professor Actual Factual had agreed to buy the fossils from Sandcrab Jones for the Bearsonian Institution. The price: five million dollars. That morning, Actual Factual had visited the discovery site to examine the bones, which Ralph and Sandcrab had stored in a big tent. Actual Factual had announced that the fossil bones belonged to a new species of meat-eater similar to *Tyrannosaurus rex*. When the whole skeleton was finally put together and displayed in the rotunda of the Hall of Dinosaurs, he predicted, it would stand fully twice as tall as a *T-rex*. Not just the science world but all Bear Country was abuzz about the spectacular new find.

"Well, let's start the meeting," said Cousin Fred when the cubs' milkshakes had been served.

"Let's wait for Ferdy," said Brother. "I invited him to join us because of his knowledge of fossils and dinosaurs." Ferdy Factual, cub genius, was Actual Factual's nephew.

"You did?" said Fred. He looked hurt. "But I know a lot about fossils and dinosaurs…"

"No offense, Fred," said Brother. "But your knowledge is all from books. Ferdy has worked with his uncle in the Bearsonian fossil lab. Real hands-on experience."

"Well, okay," said Fred. "Just so long as he keeps his hands *off* my Bear Detective spot."

Brother assured Fred that no one wanted to replace him as a permanent Bear Detective. Ferdy would only be sworn in as a temporary Bear Detective.

Moments later, Ferdy arrived. He was late because he'd come directly from the Bearsonian, where he'd had trouble getting through the crush of media bears camped outside the entrance. Brother swore him in and told him about what the cubs had seen

in the desert during the school field trip.

Ferdy stroked his chin as he listened. Then he said, "That is a very suspicious story, indeed. Ralph Ripoff and four other bears with shovels. On the day *before* Sandcrab Jones is supposed to have found the fossils. But we don't know for sure if Sandcrab was one of those bears with Ralph, or even if it was the same spot where the fossils were found."

"That's right," said Lizzy. "Maybe Ralph was out there looking for fossils in some other spot."

"That's not quite what I had in mind," said Ferdy. "It is highly unlikely that a small-time crook and swindler would become an amateur fossil hunter overnight. I was merely suggesting that before we develop any theories about what Ralph is up to, we should make sure that he was actually seen at the site of the discovery."

The cubs agreed with Ferdy and made plans to check it out. Brother thought he could find the mesa from which they'd spied Ralph. And Fred had a big map of

GREAT GRIZZLY DESERT

Great Grizzly Desert to help them. Sister thought Papa would agree to drive them out there if they told him the truth about their investigation. After all, if there was something fishy about the new fossils, it wasn't just a Bear Detective problem. It was a Bear *Country* problem.

Ferdy insisted they go the very next day, which was Saturday. There was no telling, he said, where the investigation would lead or how long it would take. Actual Factual and Ralph had already made plans to sign the bill of sale in the rotunda at the Bearsonian the following Saturday, right beside the newly put together dinosaur skeleton. So the Bear Detectives had to act fast.

"The only thing that might cause a delay in the signing," said Ferdy, "is some problem with the tests in the Bearsonian chemistry lab."

"What tests?" asked Brother.

"Uncle Actual brought a fossil toe bone back from the desert to run chemical tests on," said Ferdy. "To make sure it's a real fossil."

"You mean somebody might have made fake dinosaur fossils?" said Lizzy.

"And buried them in the desert?" said Sister.

"Well, it's highly unlikely," said Ferdy. "Not even Ralph's involvement leads me to think so. No doubt, if Ralph is involved, it's only to swindle Sandcrab Jones out of a lot of money. So the chemical tests on the *G-rex* bone are really just a precaution."

"Did you say *G-rex* bone?" asked Brother.

Ferdy blushed and put his hand to his mouth. "It just slipped out," he said. "It's supposed to be a secret, so please don't tell anyone. Uncle Actual has already decided

on a name for the new species."

"But I thought it was a new species of *Tyrannosaurus*," said Fred, eager to demonstrate his knowledge. He turned to the others. "You see," he explained, "*Tyrannosaurus* means 'tyrant lizard' in Latin, and *rex* means 'king.' King of the Tyrant Lizards. *Rex* is the species, and *Tyrannosaurus* is the genus, which is a group of related species."

"Related like brother and sister?" asked Sister.

"Related in evolution time, not family time," said Fred.

"We have family time every night after dinner," said Lizzy.

"Not *that* kind of family time!" said Fred.

"Please, Fred, allow me," Ferdy broke in. "Actually, related like brother and sister isn't such a bad way of putting it. What Fred is trying to say is that if the new species were *very* closely related to the *T-rex,* sort of like brother and sister, it would also be called *Tyrannosaurus* but would have a different name in place of *rex.* I actually suggested two such names to my uncle. I assumed he would name the creature after himself, as so many fossil hunters do. 'What about *Tyrannosaurus actualfactualus?*' I asked him. He said it was too much of a tongue-twister. 'Well, then, what about *Tyrannosaurus professorus?*' He pointed out that he wasn't the only professor in Bear Country. Then he told me that what I

G-REX

T-REX

should be trying to think up was a replacement for 'Tyrannosaurus,' not for 'rex.' Because his examination of the entire set of bones had shown that the new species was not in the same genus as *T-rex*. Now, at twice the height of *T-rex*, the new species was clearly the true king of the tyrant lizards. But, of course, that name is already taken. So I suggested *Gigantosaurus rex*. King of the Giant Lizards. Uncle agreed. And that, my friends, is how the *G-rex* was born."

"Actually, it hatched out of an egg," cracked Sister.

"Wow," breathed Fred. "Ferdy got to name the greatest of all the meat-eating dinosaurs! That must have felt awesome, Ferd!"

Ferdy faked a yawn to hide his urge to grin with embarrassing glee. "Yes," he admitted. "I did rather enjoy it."

Chapter 7
Another Field Trip

Papa Bear did agree to drive the Bear Detectives to the desert, and the very next morning they set out in the Bear family's red roadster. Their plan was simple. First, they would find the mesa from which they'd spied Ralph and the other bears. Then they would climb to the top of it and train their binoculars on the spot where the bears had been. If they could see the big tent where the *G-rex* bones were stored, then they'd know for sure that Ralph was mixed up in some shady deal involving the fossils.

The plan may have been simple, but pulling it off wasn't. Once they reached the

desert, everything looked the same. They couldn't tell one mesa from another. So they were surprised when Lizzy spoke up. "Stop here," she said, peering through her binoculars. "I think I see our mesa."

Papa insisted on going with the cubs. They had already filled their canteens from the water cooler in the trunk, so they put the top up on the roadster, locked the doors, and set off across the desert. But when they reached the top of the mesa and looked all around, nothing seemed familiar.

"What do we do now?" said Sister.

"Wait a second," said Fred. He opened

his map and spread it out on the ground. "It said in the newspaper that the fossil site is in a place called Dead Bear's Gulch. Aha! Here's Dead Bear's Gulch on the map. Now all we have to do is figure out where *we* are so we'll know what direction to go in. When we get there, we might recognize the place."

"Okay," said Sister. "So where *are* we?"

Fred examined the map for a while but got nowhere. Ferdy joined him, and they got nowhere together.

"Step aside, you two," said Papa. "It takes somebody with experience at map reading to solve a problem like this." He knelt down and studied the map for a long time. Finally, he stood up. "I've got it!" He pointed off into the distance. "See that mesa way over there?"

The cubs nodded.

"Well," said Papa, "we're right on top of it."

Sister put her hands on her hips. "Papa!" she said. "Think about what you just said!"

"Now hold on, Sis," Brother broke in. "I think the desert sun is making us all a little goofy. We'd better get back to the car before we get even more lost."

Papa agreed, and they headed for the car. But when they reached it, they couldn't get in. Papa had left the keys in the ignition.

"Is there a spare key?" asked Brother.

"Of course there is," said Papa.

"Well, where is it?" said Sister.

Papa looked at the ground and mumbled,

"Hanging from a nail in my workshop."

"That's just great!" cried Sister. "*Now* what are we gonna do? Our canteens are almost empty, and the water cooler is locked in the trunk!"

Papa and the cubs could already feel their throats going dry. They looked up to see vultures circling overhead.

But then they heard a truly wonderful sound: the drone of an engine coming down the highway.

Chapter 8
Saved!

Moments later Papa and the cubs saw that the droning engine belonged to a bus—a great big tour bus kicking up dust as it raced along the highway.

"Must be headed for Las Grizzly," said Papa. "Full of gamblers from Big Bear City."

But as the bus neared, they could make out what was printed in big letters above the windshield: DEAD BEAR'S GULCH.

"Dead Bear's Gulch?" said Brother. "Wow. Some tour company sure acted fast to cash in on the fossil find."

Papa and the cubs jumped up and down and waved. The bus pulled to a stop. Behind the wheel was a bear wearing a straw hat and green jacket.

"It's Ralph Ripoff!" said Sister. "He's organized tours to the fossil site!"

Ralph hopped down from the bus and tilted his hat against the sun's rays. "Well, well," he said. "If it isn't Papa Q. Bear and my favorite cubs. Car trouble?"

"Er...not exactly," said Papa. "*Key* trouble."

Ralph chuckled. "Locked yourselves out, did ya? Why don't you hop on the bus and take the tour? On our way back I'll tow your car. And I'll only charge you half price for the tour. Of course, I'll have to charge you the other half for the tow job. That'll be twenty dollars each. Cash or credit?"

Grumbling, Papa paid Ralph in cash. Seated next to Brother, he was still grumbling when the bus headed off down the highway again. "Your papa's a real dummy," he said. "Locking us out like that."

Ferdy leaned forward from the seat in back of them. "I disagree, Mr. Bear," he said. "In fact, it was quite a brilliant thing to do. If you hadn't locked us out, we'd be on our way home now, having accomplished nothing. But because you did, we're getting a second chance to do what we set out to do: determine if the fossil site is where Ralph was seen the other day."

Papa's frown faded. He grinned at Brother. "Ferdy has a point," he said. "I guess locking us out of the car was a pretty smart move, after all."

Chapter 9
Dead Bear's Gulch

The sun on the highway near Dead Bear's Gulch was hotter than ever. Fortunately, Ralph had put a big water cooler on the bus so the tour group could fill their canteens before setting off on their hike to the fossil site, which was almost two miles from the road.

As they hiked past a big mesa, Lizzy's sharp eyes inspected it. "That's it," she whispered to Sister. "That's the one we saw Ralph from. Pass it on."

It worked out perfectly. The mesa was about a mile from the highway, and the big tent was another mile on. The shallow gulch they'd seen before ran right by the tent. It was too dangerous to drive a big, heavy tour bus two miles off the highway, but a pickup truck could make it with ease. Now there wasn't any doubt that they'd seen Ralph and four other bears with shovels at the fossil site on the day *before* the fossils were supposed to have been discovered.

"Step right up! Step right up!" barked Ralph as he pulled a tent flap open. "See the colossal bones of the great *Gigantosaurus rex!*" Actual Factual's name for the beast had been reported that morning in every newspaper in Bear Country.

Papa and the cubs filed in with the others. It was cooler in the tent, but enough of the blazing sunlight shone through the canvas ceiling to clearly show the bones spread out on the sand.

"Wow," said Brother. "Look at the size of those things. What do you think, Papa?"

"Pretty interesting," said Papa. "Guess I'll have to bone up on dinosaurs. Get it? *Bone up on dinosaurs?*"

"I get it, Papa," said Brother. He turned to Ferdy. "More important, what do *you* think, Ferd?"

Ferdy was stroking his chin, looking thoughtfully at the vast array of fossil bones. "I think there's something fishy about these bones," he said. "They're so clean. If they've ever actually been in the ground, it couldn't have been for long." He raised his hand and called out, "Oh, Ralph!"

"That's Mr. Ripoff to you, sonny," sneered Ralph. "Oh, it's you, Ferdy. What is it, young fella?"

"Has the Bearsonian staff been here to clean off the fossils?" asked Ferdy.

"Er...uh, no, they haven't," said Ralph. "But I had Sandcrab Jones clean 'em up the other day. Wanted them to look nice and neat for the photographers." He scanned the audience. "Any other questions, folks?"

As the other tourists asked questions, the Bear Detectives huddled. "Do you think he's telling the truth?" asked Brother.

"I doubt it," said Ferdy. "But even if he is, there's something else about those bones that troubles me."

"What is it?" asked Fred.

"That's the trouble," said Ferdy. "I can't quite put my finger on it. Perhaps if I sleep on it…"

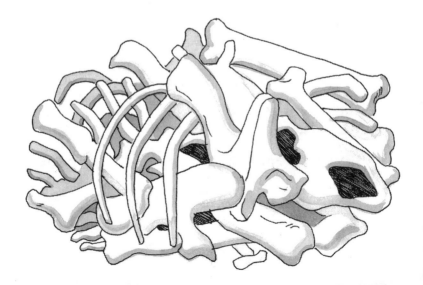

Chapter 10
Lingering Doubts

Ferdy did sleep on it. Not just for one night, though. He slept on it for *three* nights. That's because he just couldn't figure out what was bothering him about the *G-rex* fossils.

During those few days, Ferdy avoided the other Bear Detectives at school. He was embarrassed about not being able to solve a scientific problem. Finally, the others approached him in the schoolyard at recess.

"Hey, Ferdy," said Brother. "We're kind of curious about what's happening with you."

"Well," said Ferdy with a sigh, "I've gotten a lot of sleep lately, but that's about all."

"Maybe that's because there's nothing wrong with the fossils," suggested Fred.

Ferdy shook his head. "I wish it were so," he said, "but I just can't bring myself to believe it. I remain skeptical."

"*Skeptical?*" said Lizzy.

Fred, who read the dictionary for fun, defined the word. "*Skeptical,*" he said. "*Inclined to doubt or question.* It's very important for scientists to be skeptical, you know. They have to question everything until they have proof."

"Very well put," said Ferdy.

"Thanks," said Fred. "But it's also important for scientists to talk to each other about their doubts. Shouldn't you talk to your uncle about this?"

"I agree," said Ferdy. "Let's all go see him at the Bearsonian after school today."

And they did. In Actual Factual's office, Ferdy expressed his doubts about the *G-rex* fossils. The professor didn't seem to listen very carefully. When Ferdy was done, his uncle leaned back in his chair and smiled.

"Of course, as a scientist I approve of your skeptical attitude, Ferdy," said Actual Factual. "However, I must tell you that my laboratory tests on the *G-rex* toe bone are now complete. In fact, I am about to announce the results to the media. And those results show, beyond a shadow of a doubt, that the *G-rex* toe bone is chemically very similar to *T-rex* bones that are seventy million years old."

Ferdy shook his head and said, "I must admit, Uncle Actual, that this is very powerful evidence. But I still can't help wondering: if the *G-rex* lived at the same time as the *T-rex*, why haven't any fossils been found before now? A number of *T-rex* fossils have been found over the years, but not a single solitary *G-rex* bone. And now, all of a sudden, we have a whole skeleton!"

"There are any number of possible reasons for that," said the professor. "There may have been many fewer *G-rex*es than *T-rex*es. Or it may have lived in only a small space on the earth compared to *T-rex*." He smiled again. "Ah, my dear brilliant little nephew! It does my heart good to see you sticking to your guns like this. But if the lab tests can't persuade you, what can? Being skeptical is always the first thing a scientist must be. But it can be taken too far. A scientist must also be open to the new, the unexpected. Don't let your skeptical attitude ruin the excitement of this great discovery, Ferdy! Now, if you'll excuse me…"

And with that, Actual Factual strode quickly down the hall to where a crowd of reporters and photographers was waiting at the front entrance.

Chapter 11
The Unveiling

Finally, it was the day of the great unveiling—the unveiling of the put-together *G-rex* skeleton at the Bearsonian Institution. The museum staff had worked for days to piece together the great pile of bones. Now the colossal skeleton stood tall in the rotunda of the Hall of Dinosaurs, covered by an equally colossal veil of canvas. Actually, "tall" wasn't a strong enough word to describe how it stood. The top of its head almost touched the rotunda's skylight, partially blotting out the sun. It was obvious to

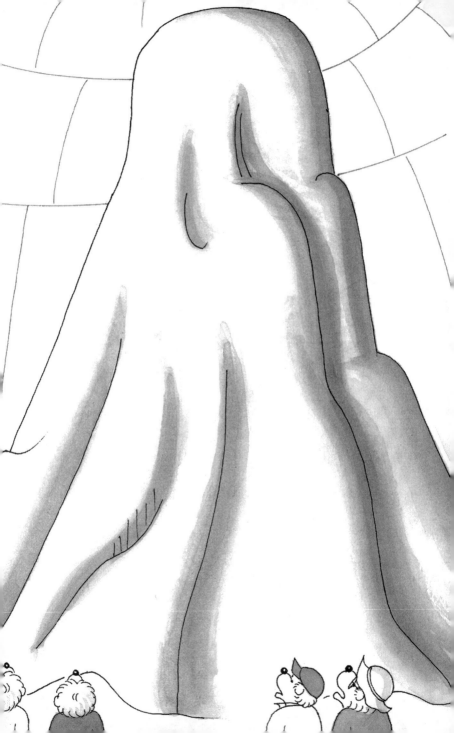

all gathered in the rotunda that the *G-rex* skeleton was fully twice the height of the big *T-rex* skeleton at the Big Bear City Museum of Natural History.

There must have been a hundred guests crammed into the rotunda. Of course, Ralph Ripoff and Sandcrab Jones were among them. So were Chief Bruno and Officer Marguerite, to maintain order and guard the *G-rex*. But the throng that circled the great covered beast was made up mostly of the media and invited scientists. The scientists wore name tags listing their universities or other institutions. Ferdy Factual, a scientist in his own right, wore a Bearsonian Institution tag. Actual Factual had given him four extra passes, which he'd given to the Bear Detectives in honor of their efforts to ensure that the *G-rex* was no hoax.

"Isn't this exciting?" said Brother to

Ferdy. "First the unveiling, then the signing." He motioned to the table that had been placed beside the *G-rex* display. "Just imagine. In a few minutes your uncle will sit there and sign the bill of sale. And the *G-rex* will belong to the Bearsonian forever."

But Ferdy didn't seem to share Brother's upbeat mood.

"What's wrong, Ferd?" asked Brother. "You don't look excited."

"That's only because I'm *not* excited," said Ferdy. "I still can't help believing that something will go wrong. Very wrong."

Brother let out a groan. "Let it go, Ferd," he pleaded. "You're gonna bring everyone else down—even your uncle..."

"Not much chance of that," scoffed Ferdy. "Uncle Actual has been lost somewhere up in the stratosphere ever since those chemical tests were completed. I'd need a guided missile to bring *him* down!"

Just then Mayor Horace J. Honeypot stepped up to the podium beside the table and spoke into the microphone. "Ladies and

gentlemen," he said in solemn tones, "we are gathered here today—"

"Is he kidding?" Sister whispered to Brother as the mayor droned on. "Does he think Actual Factual and the *G-rex* are getting married?"

"Well, in a way they are," Brother whispered back. "The *G-rex* is the greatest display in the whole museum. I'm sure the professor has a very special feeling of affection for it."

The crowd gave a thankful sigh when the mayor finally ended his boring speech and introduced Professor Actual Factual. They gave the professor a standing ovation. (Of course, they were already standing, anyway.)

"Thank you, friends, Beartowners, and visiting scientists," said Actual Factual. "As much as I'd like to, I won't bore you with a long scientific lecture about *Gigantosaurus rex.* Suffice it to say that the great creature clearly lived up to its name. And now, without further ado, here's what you've all been waiting for: the unveiling!"

Actual Factual signaled to the workbears who were in charge of the great ropes tied to the veil. They pulled on the ropes and down came the veil, landing in a crumpled heap at the skeleton's huge bony feet.

A hundred gasps could be heard as a hundred pairs of eyes lifted toward the skylight. The massive feet, legs, chest, and tail all made quite an impression on the audience. But what instantly drew everyone's attention was the immense head. The great jaws were slightly open, as if the beast were gathering breath for a monstrous roar.

"Wow!" said Sister, shivering a little.

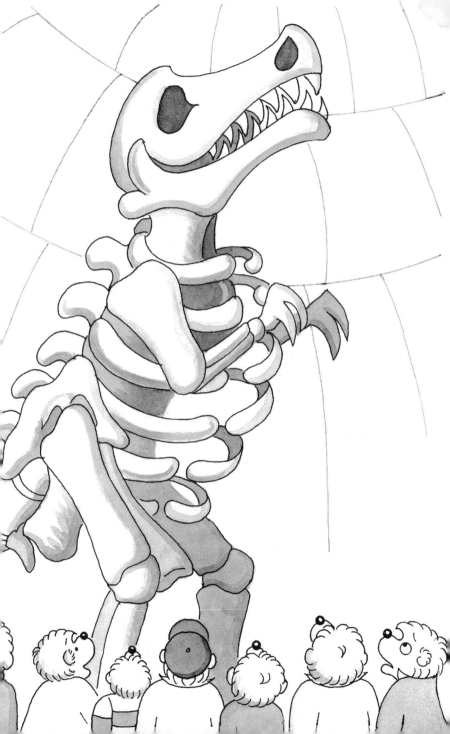

"What huge teeth it has!"

"All the better to eat you with," teased Fred.

"But what *tiny* hands it has!" added Sister.

"All the better to pick its teeth with after it eats you," said Fred.

"Cut it out!" snapped Sister. "You're scaring me!"

"Okay, Fred, cool it," Brother cautioned. He turned to Ferdy. "Well, what do you think now, Ferdy?"

But Ferdy didn't even hear him. His gaze was set on the *G-rex,* and a frown was fixed on his face. He was lost in deepest thought.

Lizzy, Bear Country's biggest nature lover, had been speechless until now. "My goodness!" she gasped. "It's a magnificent creature! What a shame it went extinct!"

"A *shame?*" said Sister. "You gotta be kiddin', Liz! I'm *glad* that big ugly thing is extinct! If it wasn't, I'd move to another planet!"

At last the hushed crowd found its voice. Its hands, too. It broke into applause, with cries of "Bravo!" and "Magnificent!"

Twirling his cane, Ralph Ripoff came forward to place a sheet of paper on the table. He motioned for quiet. "Don't mean to break up the party, folks," he said. "But the

time has come for what *I've* been waiting for: the signing. Gentlemen, if you would please take your places…"

There were two chairs at the table. Actual Factual sat in one, Sandcrab Jones in the other.

"Mr. Jones," said Ralph, handing the old hermit a pen, "if you would sign first, please." He pointed to the spot on the bill of sale. But Sandcrab just stared at it. He motioned Ralph to lean closer and whispered in his ear.

"Well, then," said Ralph, "in that case, just make your mark."

Sandcrab smiled a toothless smile and drew a little picture of a crab on the line meant for his signature. He handed the pen to Actual Factual.

"And now, Professor," said Ralph, with barely controlled glee, "if you would put

your 'Actual Factual' right here on the dotted line…"

The professor placed the point of the pen
on the dotted line and began to write.

Suddenly, a cub's voice echoed through
the rotunda. "Stop! Don't sign it!"

All eyes turned to the speaker. It was Ferdy. He dashed to the *G-rex* and pulled a tape measure from his pocket. He measured the width of a leg bone and looked over at his uncle with alarm. "You mustn't sign it, Uncle Actual!" he cried. He hurried to the table, leaned over it, and whispered something in Actual Factual's ear. As the professor listened, his eyes grew wide.

"I most certainly will *not* sign!" announced Actual Factual, jumping to his feet. He pointed accusingly at the great bony creature. "This so-called fossil skeleton is not a *G-rex!* In fact, it isn't a fossil skeleton at all! It is a *hoax!*"

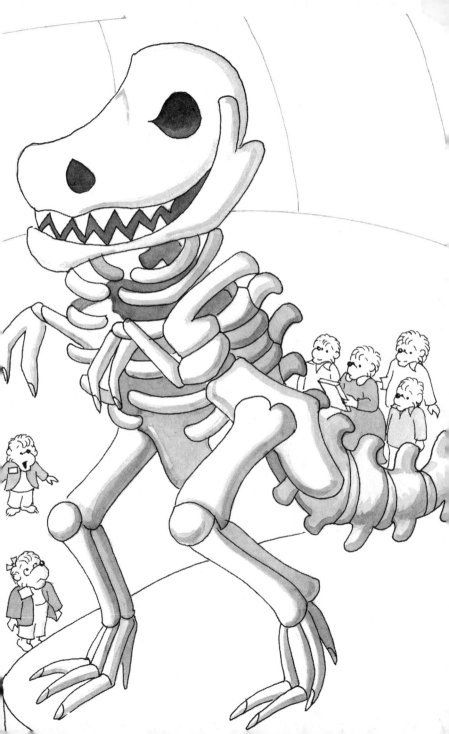

Chapter 12
King of the Giant Hoaxes

At Actual Factual's shocking announcement, a nervous murmur rippled through the crowd in the rotunda.

"How do you know it's a hoax, Professor?" shouted a reporter.

"Because of what my brilliant nephew,

Ferdy Factual, just pointed out to me," said the professor. "I should have seen it myself, of course, but I've been so wrapped up in the chemical tests that I just didn't notice it. Perhaps I was also so excited about this great discovery that I didn't *want* to notice it. Ferdy, why don't you explain it to the audience?"

Ferdy stepped to the podium and disappeared behind it. Quickly, Actual Factual moved a chair behind the podium for Ferdy to stand on. When the cub's face reappeared, it was beaming with pride at the chance to show off in front of the media and fellow scientists.

"I observed the fossil bones out at Dead Bear's Gulch," said Ferdy, "but it didn't occur to me then. It wasn't until I saw the skeleton all put together that it hit me. The *G-rex* is twice the height of the largest *T-rex* ever found. But it has the same basic body shape as *T-rex*, which means that its *weight* must have been much greater than twice that of *T-rex*. That we know from the basic laws of physics. And yet the *G-rex* bones are only *twice as thick* as *T-rex*'s." He pointed to the towering skeleton. "Those bones could never support the weight of that body. In fact, it would be *impossible* for a creature with *G-rex*'s body shape to reach such a height. Its bones would have to be so thick that there would be no room left for flesh or internal organs. Thus, we know that whoever planned this hoax was neither a biologist nor a physicist."

"An excellent observation, Ferdy," said Actual Factual as he replaced his nephew at the microphone. "What strikes me is that the chemical makeup of the phony fossils is so accurate. There must have been a very brilliant chemist involved in this hoax…"

The professor broke off and stared into space for a long moment. Suddenly, his eyes lit up. "I know who it was!" he cried. He scanned the audience until his gaze came to rest on a bearded scientist wearing a name tag that read: DR. REX GIANT, BIG BEAR UNIVERSITY. He pointed directly at the scientist and cried, "It was he! Seize him!"

Several scientists took hold of their colleague's arms as Actual Factual strode to meet him. "Rex Giant!" he said. *"Gigantosaurus rex,* Rex Giant. Very funny, Zoltan."

The audience gasped as the professor reached up and ripped off the bear's beard and mustache. Of course, they came off easily because they were as phony as he was.

Actual Factual smiled. "Dr. Bearish, I

presume! I didn't recognize you without your silly hat and ugly coat."

Dr. Zoltan Bearish glared back at Actual Factual, his penetrating gaze boring into the professor's mind like an electric drill. Quickly, Actual Factual turned away to address the crowd.

"This is the brilliant chemist who worked for me at the Bearsonian five years ago," he said. "He spent more time on his own private experiments than on the work I gave him. And his carelessness ruined one of my most important experiments. So I fired him. Obviously, he planned this hoax to get revenge."

All of a sudden, Sandcrab Jones was on his knees before Actual Factual, pleading with the professor. "Please!" he wailed. "Don't send me to jail! I confess to everything! Ralph Ripoff paid me to 'discover'

those phony bones at Dead Bear's Gulch. I needed the money to fix my shack because that lousy termite insurance Ralph sold me wouldn't pay!"

"He's lying!" cried Ralph as Officer Marguerite put him in an armlock. "The old coot's feeble-minded! He doesn't know what he's saying!"

"It's true!" said Sandcrab. "Ralph paid me thirty dollars!"

"Thirty dollars?" shouted Dr. Bearish. "Why, you swindler, Ripoff! You told me you paid him *two hundred* dollars!"

"*You're* calling *me* a swindler?" cried Ralph.

"Enough quarreling!" said Actual Factual. "You three can settle your scores in prison! Arrest them all, Chief!"

But instead of arresting anyone, Chief Bruno stepped forward and gently helped

Sandcrab Jones to his feet. "Rest easy, old-timer," he said. "Nobody's going to prison. Let go of Ralph, Marguerite. And the rest of you unhand Dr. Bearish."

"What?" cried Actual Factual. "Let them go? But this is the cruelest hoax in the history of Bear Country! It's a clear case of *fraud!*"

Chief Bruno shook his head and said calmly, "What you mean, Professor, is that it's a clear case of *almost* fraud." He went to the signing table and held up the bill of sale. "Professor, you put your 'Actual' on the dotted line, but not your 'Factual.' That means *no sale*. No sale, no fraud. Thus, no crime. Bear Country has anti-fraud laws, but no anti-*almost*-fraud laws."

The crowd began to grumble. Then there were boos and hisses. Clearly, they didn't agree with Chief Bruno.

BUT UNCLE ACTUAL, YOU ARE A ROCKET SCIENTIST.

But Actual Factual signaled for quiet. "Now wait just a second, everyone," he said. "The chief is right. It doesn't take a rocket scientist to see that."

"But Uncle Actual," said Ferdy, "you *are* a rocket scientist."

"Oh, yes, I forgot," said the professor. "What I mean is: the chief is obviously correct in his legal analysis of the situation. We'll just have to be content that Ferdy uncovered the hoax through his powers of observation and his knowledge of the laws of physics." He looked again at the towering *G-rex* skeleton and turned to his nephew. "You know, Ferdy, I'm a bit surprised that those flimsy bones are strong enough even

to support their *own* weight..."

No sooner were the words out of the professor's mouth than a spooky creaking sound echoed through the rotunda.

"Look out!" someone cried. "Head for the halls!"

But there was no time for anyone to get out of the rotunda. In a matter of seconds, the entire *G-rex* skeleton buckled, toppled in on itself, and came crashing to the floor. The rotunda was littered with the shattered pieces. A great cloud of bone dust filled the air. *Fake* bone dust, that is.

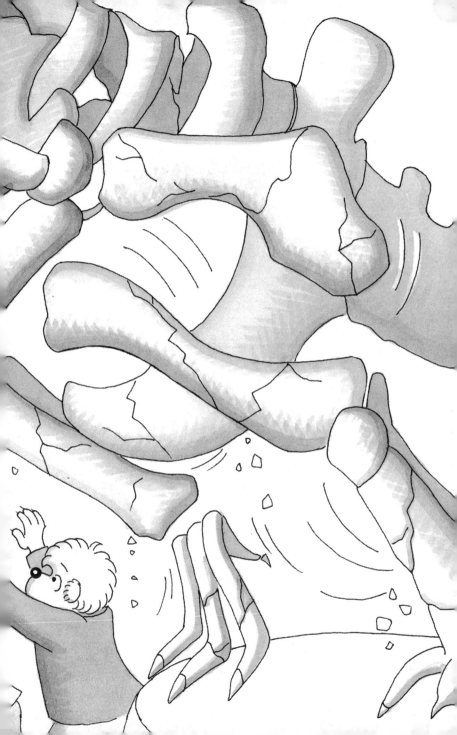

Fortunately, no one was injured. As everyone brushed the dust from their clothes, Actual Factual said into the microphone, "At this time, I would like to rename the exhibit. It is *Outrageous rex*: King of the Giant Hoaxes!"

Now the rotunda filled with laughter as well as fake bone dust.

And so ends the tale of the *G-rex* bones. *Fake G-rex* bones, that is. Actual Factual

was almost sorry to see the debris from the shattered skeleton cleared away. Because that left the rotunda empty once more. Ferdy told him not to be discouraged, that someday he might find a *real G-rex*. But, of course, Actual Factual knew that that was impossible. For the *G-rex* was not just an imaginary creature. It was an *impossible* imaginary creature.

Actual Factual could only hope for the

possible. So he hoped for the day when a complete *T-rex* skeleton would grace the rotunda in the Hall of Dinosaurs.

And to this day he is still looking for one. And still hoping.

Stan and Jan Berenstain began writing and illustrating books for children in the early 1960s, when their two young sons were beginning to read. That marked the start of the best-selling Berenstain Bears series. Now, with more than one hundred books in print, videos, television shows, and even Berenstain Bears attractions at major amusement parks, it's hard to tell where the Bears end and the Berenstains begin!

Stan and Jan make their home in Bucks County, Pennsylvania, near their sons—Leo, a writer, and Michael, an illustrator—who are helping them with Big Chapter Books stories and pictures. They plan on writing and illustrating many more books for children, especially for their four grandchildren, who keep them well in touch with the kids of today.